Claus Stamm

Three Strong Women

A TALL TALE FROM JAPAN

Pictures by
Jean and Mou-sien Tseng

VIKING

VIKING
Published by the Penguin Group
Viking Penguin, a division of Penguin Books USA Inc.,
40 West 23rd Street, New York, New York 10010, U.S.A.
Penguin Books Ltd, 27 Wrights Lane, London W8 5TZ, England
Penguin Books Australia Ltd, Ringwood, Victoria, Australia
Penguin Books Canada Ltd, 2801 John Street, Markham, Ontario, Canada L3R 1B4
Penguin Books (N.Z.) Ltd, 182–190 Wairau Road, Auckland 10, New Zealand

Penguin Books Ltd, Registered Offices: Harmondsworth, Middlesex, England

First published in 1962 by the Viking Press.
This edition with new illustrations published in 1990
1   3   5   7   9   10   8   6   4   2

Library of Congress Cataloging-in-Publication Data
Stamm, Claus.   Three strong women /
Claus Stamm ; illustrated by Jean and Mou-sien Tseng   p.   cm.
Summary: When the famous wrestler Forever Mountain tickles a plump little girl,
the consequence is that he must be trained by her, her mother, and her grandmother.
ISBN 0-670-83323-1
[1. Fairy tales.   2. Folklore—Japan.]   I. Tseng, Jean, ill.
II. Tseng, Mou-Sien, ill.   III. Title.
PZ8.S48Th 1990   398.21'0952—dc20   89-48758

Printed in Japan
Set in Novarese Medium

For
Dr. Seiler, Dr. Payson
and
the Beekman Downtown Hospital
in order of their appearance

Long ago, in Japan, there lived a famous wrestler. One day he decided to make his way to the capital city to wrestle before the Emperor.

He strode down the road on legs thick as the trunks of small trees. He had been walking for seven hours and could walk for seven more without getting tired. The time was autumn.

The wrestler hummed to himself, "Zun-zun-zun," in time with the long swing of his legs. Wind blew through his thin brown robe, and he wore no sword at his side. He needed no sword, even in the darkest and loneliest places, and few tailors would have been able to make warm clothes for a man so broad and tall. He felt strong, healthy, and rather conceited.

He thought: "They call me Forever-Mountain because I am a good wrestler. I'm a fine, brave man and far too modest ever to say so. . . ."

Just then he saw a girl who must have come up from the nearby river, for she steadied a bucket on her head. Her hands on the bucket were small, and there was a dimple on each thumb. She was a round little girl with red cheeks and a nose like a friendly button. Her eyes looked as though she were thinking of ten thousand funny stories at once. She clambered up onto the road and walked ahead of the wrestler.

"If I don't tickle that fat girl, I shall regret it all my life," said the wrestler to himself. "She will squeak and I shall laugh and laugh. If she drops her bucket, I can run and fill it again and carry it home for her."

He tiptoed up and poked her lightly in the ribs.

"Kochokochokocho!" he said, a fine, ticklish sound in Japanese.

The girl gave a satisfying squeal, giggled, and brought one arm down so that the wrestler's hand was caught between it and her body.

"Ho-ho-ho! You've caught me! I can't move at all!" said the wrestler.

"I know," said the jolly girl.

He felt that it was very good-tempered of her to take a joke so well, and started to pull his hand free. Somehow, he could not.

He tried again, using a little more strength.

"Now, now—let me go, little girl," he said. "I am a powerful man. If I pull hard I might hurt you."

"Pull," said the girl. "I admire powerful men."

She began to walk, and though the wrestler tugged and pulled until his feet dug great furrows in the ground, he had to follow.

Ten minutes later, still tugging while trudging helplessly after her, he was glad that the road was lonely and no one was there to see.

"Please let me go," he pleaded. "I am the famous wrestler Forever-Mountain. I must go show my strength before the Emperor"—he burst out weeping from shame and confusion—"and you're hurting my hand!"

The girl steadied the bucket on her head with her free hand and dimpled sympathetically over her shoulder. "You poor, sweet little Forever-Mountain," she said. "Are you tired? Shall I carry you?

"I do not want you to carry me. I want you to let me go. I want to forget I ever saw you. What do you want with me?" moaned the pitiful wrestler.

"I only want to help you," said the girl, now pulling him steadily up and up a narrow mountain path. "Oh, I am sure you'll have no more trouble than anyone else against the other wrestlers. You'll win, or else you'll lose, and you won't be too badly hurt either way. But aren't you afraid you might meet a really *strong* man someday?"

Forever-Mountain turned white. He stumbled. He was imagining being laughed at throughout Japan as "Hardly-Ever-Mountain."

She glanced back.

"You see? Tired already," she said. "I'll walk more slowly. Why don't you come along to my mother's house and let us make a strong man of you? The wrestling in the capital won't begin for three months. I know, because Grandmother thought she'd go. You'd be spending all that time in bad company and wasting what little power you have."

"All right. Three months. I'll come," said the wrestler. He felt he had nothing more to lose. Also, he feared that the girl might be angry if he refused, and place him in the top of a tree until he changed his mind.

"Fine," she said happily. "We are almost there."

She freed his hand. It was red and a little swollen. "But if you break your promise and run off, I'll have to chase you and carry you back."

Soon they arrived in a small valley where a simple farmhouse with a thatched roof stood.

"Grandmother is at home, but she is an old lady and she's probably sleeping." The girl shaded her eyes with one hand. "But Mother should be bringing our cow back from the field. There's Mother now!"

She waved. The woman coming around the corner of the house put down the cow she was carrying and waved back.

She smiled and came across the grass, walking with a lively bounce like her daughter's. Well, maybe her bounce was a little more solid, thought the wrestler.

"Excuse me," she said. "These mountain paths are full of stones. They hurt the cow's feet. And who is the nice young man, Maru-me?"

The girl explained. "And we have only three months!" she finished anxiously.

"Well, it's not long enough to do much, but it's not so short a time that we can't do something," said her mother, looking thoughtful. "But he does look terribly feeble. He'll need a lot of good things to eat. Maybe he can help Grandmother with some of the easy housework."

"That will be fine!" said the girl, and she called her grandmother—loudly, for the old lady was a little deaf.

"I'm coming!" came a creaky voice from inside the house, and a little old woman leaning on a stick tottered out of the door. As she came toward them she stumbled over the roots of a great oak tree.

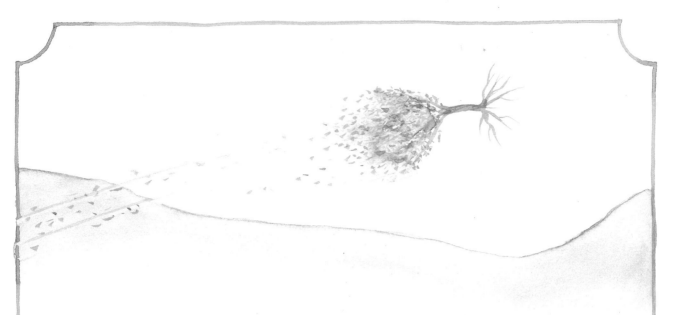

"Heh! My eyes aren't what they used to be. That's the fourth time this month I've stumbled over that tree," she complained and, wrapping her skinny arms about its trunk, pulled it out of the ground.

"Oh, Grandmother! You should have let me pull it up for you," said Maru-me.

"Hm. I hope I didn't hurt my poor old back," muttered the old lady. She called out, "Daughter! Throw that tree away like a good girl, so no one will fall over it. But make sure it doesn't hit anybody."

"You can help Mother with the tree," Maru-me said to Forever-Mountain. "On second thought, you'd better not help. Just watch."

Her mother went to the tree, picked it up in her two hands, and threw it—clumsily and with a little gasp.

Up went the tree, sailing end over end, growing smaller and smaller as it flew. It landed with a faint crash far up the mountainside.

"Ah, how clumsy," she said. "I meant to throw it *over* the mountain. It's probably blocking the path now, and I'll have to move it tomorrow."

The wrestler was not listening. He had very quietly fainted.

"Oh! We must put him to bed," said Maru-me.

"Poor, feeble young man," said her mother.

"I hope we can do something for him. Here, let me carry him, he's light," said the grandmother. She slung him over her shoulder and carried him into the house, creaking along with her cane.

The next day they began the work of making Forever-Mountain over into what they thought a strong man should be. They gave him the simplest food to eat, and the toughest. Day by day they prepared his rice with less and less water, until no ordinary man could have chewed or digested it.

Every day he was made to do the work of five men, and every evening he wrestled with Grandmother. Maru-me and her mother agreed that Grandmother, being old and feeble, was the least likely to injure him accidentally. They hoped the exercise might be good for her rheumatism.

He grew stronger and stronger but was hardly aware of it. Grand-mother could still throw him easily into the air—and catch him again—without ever changing her sweet old smile.

He quite forgot that outside this valley he was one of the greatest wrestlers in Japan and was called Forever-Mountain. His legs had been like logs; now they were like pillars. His big hands were hard as stones, and when he cracked his knuckles the sound was like trees splitting on a cold night.

Sometimes he did an exercise that wrestlers do in Japan—raising one foot high above the gound and bringing it down with a crash. Then people in nearby villages looked up at the winter sky and said that it was very late in the year for thunder.

Soon he could pull up a tree as well as the grandmother. He could even throw one—but only a small distance. One evening, near the end of his third month, he wrestled with Grandmother and held her down for half a minute.

"Heh-heh!" She chortled and got up, smiling with every wrinkle. "I'd never have believed it!"

Maru-me squealed with joy and threw her arms around him—gently, for she was afraid of cracking his ribs.

"Very good, very good! What a strong man," said her mother, who had just come home from the fields, carrying, as usual, the cow. She put the cow down and patted the wrestler on the back.

They agreed that he was now ready to show some *real* strength before the Emperor.

"Take the cow along with you tomorrow when you go," said the mother. "Sell her and buy yourself a belt—a silken belt. Buy the fattest and heaviest one you can find. Wear it when you appear before the Emperor, as a souvenir from us."

"I wouldn't think of taking your only cow. You've already done too much for me. And you'll need her to plow the fields, won't you?"

They burst out laughing. Maru-me squealed, her mother roared. The grandmother cackled so hard and long that she choked and had to be pounded on the back.

"Oh, dear," said the mother, still laughing. "You didn't think we used our cow for *work*! Why, Grandmother here is stronger than five cows!"

"The cow is our pet," Maru-me giggled. "She has lovely brown eyes."

"But it really gets tiresome having to carry her back and forth each day so that she has enough grass to eat," said her mother.

"Then you must let me give you all the prize money that I win," said Forever-Mountain.

"Oh, no! We wouldn't think of it!" said Maru-me. "Because we all like you too much to sell you anything. And it is not proper to accept gifts of money from strangers."

"True," said Forever-Mountain. "I will now ask your mother's and grandmother's permission to marry you. I want to be one of the family."

"Oh! I'll make a wedding dress!" said Maru-me.

The mother and grandmother pretended to consider very seriously, but they quickly agreed.

Next morning Forever-Mountain tied his hair up in the topknot that all Japanese wrestlers wear, and got ready to leave. He thanked Maru-me and her mother and bowed very low to the grandmother, since she was the oldest and had been a fine wrestling partner. Then he picked up the cow and trudged up the mountain. When he reached the top, he slung the cow over one shoulder and waved good-bye to Maru-me.

At the first town he came to, Forever-Mountain sold the cow. She brought a good price because she was unusually fat from never having worked in her life. With the money, he bought the heaviest silken belt he could find.

When he reached the palace grounds, many of the other wrestlers were already there, sitting about, eating enormous bowls of rice, comparing one another's weight, and telling stories. They paid little attention to Forever-Mountain, except to wonder why he had arrived so late this year. Some of them noticed that he had grown very quiet and took no part at all in their boasting.

All the ladies and gentlemen of the court were waiting in a special courtyard for the wrestling to begin. They wore many robes, one on top of another, heavy with embroidery and gold cloth, and sweat ran down their faces and froze in the winter afternoon. The gentlemen had long swords so weighted with gold and precious stones that they could never have used them, even if they had known how. The court ladies, with their long black hair hanging down behind, had their faces painted dead white, which made them look frightened. They had pulled out their real eyebrows and painted new ones high above the place where eyebrows are supposed to be, and this made them all look as though they were very surprised at something.

Behind a screen sat the Emperor—by himself, because he was too noble for ordinary people to look at. He was a lonely old man with a kind, tired face. He hoped the wrestling would end quickly so that he could go to his room and write poems.

The first two wrestlers chosen to fight were Forever-Mountain and a wrestler who was said to have the biggest stomach in the country. He and Forever-Mountain both threw some salt into the ring. It was said that this drove away evil spirits.

Then the other wrestler, moving his stomach somewhat out of the way, raised his foot and brought it down with a fearful stamp. He glared fiercely at Forever-Mountain as if to say, "Now *you* stamp, you poor frightened man!"

Forever-Mountain raised his foot. He brought it down.

There was a sound like thunder, the earth shook, and the other wrestler bounced into the air and out of the ring, as gracefully as any soap bubble.

He picked himself up and bowed to the Emperor's screen.

"The earth-god is angry. Possibly there is something the matter with the salt," he said. "I do not think I shall wrestle this season." And he walked out, looking very suspiciously over one shoulder at Forever-Mountain.

Five other wrestlers then and there decided that they were not wrestling this season, either.

From then on, Forever-Mountain brought his foot down lightly. As each wrestler came into the ring, he picked him up very gently, carried him out, and placed him before the Emperor's screen, bowing most courteously every time.

The court ladies' eyebrows went up even higher. The gentlemen looked disturbed and a little afraid. They loved to see fierce, strong men tugging and grunting at each other, but Forever-Mountain was a little too much for them. Only the Emperor was happy. With the wrestling over so quickly, he would have that much more time to write his poems. He ordered all the prize money handed over to Forever-Mountain.

"But," he said, "you had better not wrestle any more." He stuck a finger through his screen and waggled it at the other wrestlers, who were sitting on the ground weeping with disappointment like great fat babies.

Forever-Mountain promised not to wrestle any more. Everybody looked relieved. The wrestlers sitting on the ground almost smiled.

"I think I shall become a farmer," Forever-Mountain said.

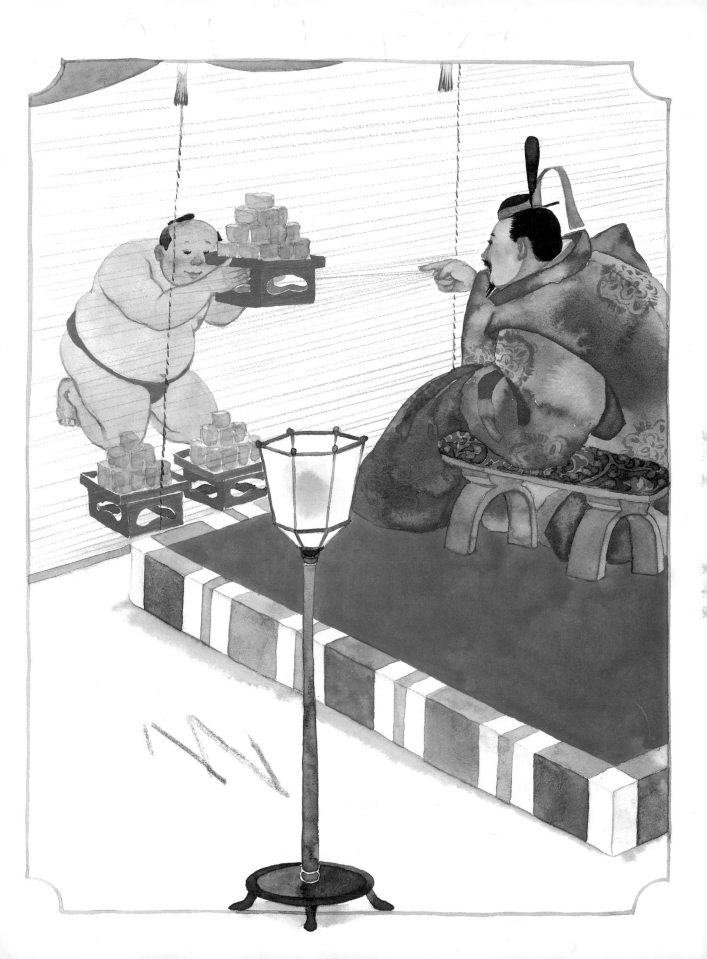

Maru-me was waiting for him. When she saw him coming, she ran down the mountain, picked him up, together with the heavy bags of prize money, and carried him halfway up the mountainside. Then she giggled and put him down. The rest of the way she let him carry her.

Forever-Mountain kept his promise to the Emperor and never fought in public again. His name was forgotten in the capital. But up in the mountains, sometimes, the earth shakes and rumbles, and they say that it is Forever-Mountain and Maru-me's grandmother practicing wrestling.